Adventures in Janja

Tales of Mr. & Mrs. Rwego

©Simon Nzubahimana

Manchester 2023.

First edition,

Manchester, UK, 2023

ISBN- 9798860289185

Order your copy from amazon.com.

Table of Contents

Preface..7

Story 1: The Fiery Comb Debate 9

Story 2: The Magic Maize Maze 11

Story 3: Mrs. Rwego's Talking Chicken..................14

Story 4: The Moonlight Dance 17

Story 5: The Stream's Riddle 20

Story 6: Mysterious Footprints 22

Story 8: Mrs. Rwego's Magic Potion 28

Story 9: Festival of Harvest......................................30

Story 10: Whispering Winds 32

Story 11: The Golden Egg 35

Story 12: The Day Janja Turned Colourful 38

Story 13: Shadows in the Night..............................40

Story 14: The Tale of Akavumbura.........................43

Story 15: The Village Time Capsule.......................46

Story 18 The Tale of the Tailless Frog 53

Story 19: The Dinner Dilemma in Janja"...............55

Story 20: Peter's Day at Home 58

Story 21: George's Silly Adventures 61

Story 22: Goodbye, Janja..63

Preface

Nestled in the verdant landscapes of North East England lies a quaint, remote village named Janja. It is here that our story unfolds, centring around a warm and vibrant African family. Surrounded by the chirping of birds and the gentle rustling of leaves, the family lives harmoniously with an array of animals and pets, each adding their unique essence to the tales that will follow.

Janja, being remote, stands at a distance from the luxuries of modern-day conveniences. The hum of the internet and the warmth of gas pipelines are foreign to its inhabitants. Yet, they find solace and energy in the coal that burns in their hearths, casting a warm, amber glow on their faces during the chilly nights.

But Janja is not just about its remoteness; it is a land of abundance. Beehives buzz with activity, producing the sweetest honey, fields blush with the red of beetroot, and the earth hides treasures of potatoes. Towering maize plants dance to the whims of the wind, while cows, horses, and chickens add to the cacophony of rural life.

Each morning, the family embarks on a journey, driving their children 15 miles through winding roads and picturesque landscapes to the nearest school. And as the sun dips below the horizon, marking the end of another day, the family gathers. With the stars as their audience and the night as their stage, the children find solace in the world of stories. From tales passed down through generations to the ones freshly inked by their parents, every evening is a new adventure.

This book is a tribute to those evenings, a collection of stories that have warmed the hearts of the children of Janja. They are tales of love, adventure, lessons, and dreams. It is our hope that, as you turn these pages, you too will be transported to Janja, feeling the warmth of the coal hearth and the magic of the stories that unfold.

May this book serve as a cherished tool for parents and children alike, bringing joy, wonder, and a touch of Janja's magic to all who read it.

STORY 1: THE FIERY COMB DEBATE

  One sunny day in Janja, the village children gathered around to witness an unusual sight: a conversation between Kuku, the rooster, and Fisi, the cunning fox.

Fisi, always curious and somewhat mischievous, approached Kuku with a question, "Why do you have that funny red comb atop your head, Kuku?"

Kuku, aware of Fisi's sly nature and not wanting to become his next meal, replied, "Ah, Fisi! This is not just a comb. It contains the fiercest fire known to all of Janja. It protects me from those who wish me harm."

Fisi scoffed, "Fire? In that tiny thing? I don't believe you."

Kuku responded confidently, "Would you like a touch? But be warned, it might just burn you!"

Fisi's eyes widened. He'd heard tales from other animals about getting burned, and he certainly didn't want to experience it firsthand. He hesitated, looking at the comb, then back to Kuku's sly smile.

The village children giggled watching the once cunning fox, unsure and doubtful.

"Maybe another day," Fisi replied, trying to keep his pride, "I have other matters to attend to."

And with that, the fox retreated, and Kuku, with his fiery comb, became the talk of Janja, illustrating how wit can sometimes be mightier than strength.

Proverb at the End: "Wisdom is like a baobab tree; no one individual can embrace it."

Story 2: The Magic Maize Maze

It was a bright and sunny day in the village of Janja. Children's laughter filled the air as they played tag, their feet kicking up little clouds of dust. Among them were Amina, Jengo, and little Lulu. While chasing Lulu, Amina and Jengo stumbled upon something they had never seen before - a massive entrance made of golden maize plants. Curiosity twinkling in their eyes, they peered inside and saw a winding pathway.

«This isn't just any maize field. It's a maze!» whispered Jengo, his voice filled with awe.

Lulu, being the youngest and most adventurous, darted in without a second thought. «Come catch me!» she squealed with joy.

Realising they couldn't leave little Lulu alone inside, Amina and Jengo ventured in after her, their hearts filled with both excitement and trepidation.

The maize stood tall, their tassels brushing against the sky. Sunlight filtered through, casting golden patterns on the ground. As the children explored deeper into the maze, they started noticing peculiar things. Symbols and patterns on some maize leaves, soft whispers carried by the wind, and a faint shimmer in the air.

Suddenly, Amina took a turn and found herself at a dead end with an inscribed stone. It read, «To move forward, sometimes you need to take a step back.»

Jengo, in another part of the maze, found a similar stone which read, «The journey matters more than the destination.»

Meanwhile, Lulu, with her tiny feet and giggling at every turn, found a stone that simply said, «Laugh, and the path will appear.»

Lost and intrigued, the children almost forgot the way out until Mr. Rwego's familiar voice echoed through the maze, «Children! Follow my voice, and remember the lessons of the maze.»

The trio, relying on the wisdom of the stones and the guidance of Mr. Rwego's voice, finally found their way to the centre of the maze. There, in a clearing, stood Mr. Rwego, with a knowing smile on his face.

«You found the heart of the maize maze!» He declared. «Every turn, every challenge in this maze holds a lesson, much like in life.»

The children, catching their breath and their hearts full of newfound wisdom, nodded in agreement.

They realised that the maze was not just about finding their way out, but about understanding life's lessons: patience, resilience, joy, and the guidance of elders.

And as the golden sunset of Janja painted the sky, the children left the maize maze, knowing they had experienced a magical journey, both within and outside.

Proverb at the End: «Life is a journey, and every path has its puddle.»

Story 3: Mrs. Rwego's Talking Chicken

The village of Janja was always alive with whispers and stories, but one morning, the loudest whisper wasn't from the village children or the babbling brook. It was from a chicken, specifically Mrs. Rwego's favourite chicken, whom she affectionately named Koko.

Now, Koko was no ordinary chicken. She had bright, observant eyes and a keen sense of everything happening around her. On this particular day, as Mrs. Rwego fed the chickens, Koko strutted up to her and, to Mrs. Rwego's astonishment, said, «Good morning, Mrs. Rwego! Did you know Amina borrowed Jengo's toy yesterday and hasn't returned it?»

Mrs. Rwego, taken aback, replied, «Koko, since when do you talk? And why are you concerned with children's matters?»

Koko clucked humorously, «I have always been talkative. Just no one listened! And as for the children's matters, well, I see everything from my roost.»

Throughout the day, Koko spilled more secrets, much to the amusement of Mrs. Rwego.

«Kaguru told her little brother that the moon is made of cheese,» Koko reported during lunchtime.

By evening, word had spread about Koko's newfound voice, and the village children gathered around Mrs. Rwego's house, eager to hear what the chicken might say about them.

Koko did not disappoint. «Ali Baba tried to bake a cake for his mother's birthday but forgot the sugar!» she clucked, resulting in giggles from the gathered crowd. «And Sitini? She secretly danced in the rain when she thought no one was watching.»

Each revelation was met with blushes, gasps, or laughter, but most importantly, with confessions.

«It's true,» Amina sighed, «I did borrow Jengo's toy. I'll return it tomorrow.»

Ali Baba sheepishly grinned, «I will remember the sugar next time.»

Mrs. Rwego, seeing an opportunity for a lesson, gathered the children around and said, «See, little secrets aren't necessarily harmful, but it's always good to be honest. Imagine if all our chickens started talking?!»

The children nodded, their faces reflecting newfound realisations.

And just as the sun was setting, Koko, with a mischievous gleam in her eyes, whispered to Mrs. Rwego, «I might just tell them about the time you accidentally watered the plants with soup.»

Mrs. Rwego laughed heartily, replying, «Ah, Koko, honesty truly is the best policy!»

Proverb at the End: «Truth's nest is on an open field.»

Story 4: The Moonlight Dance

The village of Janja, with its mud-brick houses and fields of gold, was a wonder during the day, but it was during the full moon nights that its real magic shone through. Those nights, under the silvery glow of the moon, were special – they were the nights of the Moonlight Dance.

As dusk approached, a palpable excitement spread throughout Janja. Children ran about, helping set up the village square with lanterns and drums. The elders, with their rich stories and ancient songs, settled on mats, ready to guide the younger generations through the night.

On this particular moonlit night, Mr. & Mrs. Rwego took centre stage. They wore traditional attire, vibrant and rich with history – garments passed down through generations. Mr. Rwego's deep voice echoed across the square, «Tonight, we dance not just to the rhythm of the drums, but to the heartbeat of our ancestors.»

Mrs. Rwego clapped her hands, and the drums began their hypnotic beat. «Watch and learn,» she said, her eyes gleaming with pride.

The dance started slow, with deliberate movements, telling tales of the earth and its bounty. Then, as the rhythm picked up, it transitioned into tales of valiant warriors, gracious queens, and timeless love stories.

Jengo tried to mimic Mr. Rwego, his feet stumbling a bit, but his spirit undeterred. Amina and Lulu followed Mrs. Rwego, their laughter mixing with the rhythmic beats, creating a melody of past and present.
As the night progressed, stories unfolded not just through dance, but also through songs sung by the village elders. Tales of bravery, wisdom, love, and hope were passed down, ensuring that the traditions and tales of yore were not forgotten.

Kaguru, a young boy of Janja, with twinkling eyes, asked, «Why do we dance, Mrs. Rwego?»

She smiled warmly, taking a brief pause, «We dance, dear Kaguru, to remember and to teach. We dance to celebrate our past and to hope for our future. We dance to unite – every step, every clap, every laugh brings Janja together.»
As dawn approached, with tired feet but elated hearts, the village of Janja concluded their Moonlight Dance. They had, under the watchful eyes of the moon, kept the traditions alive, ensuring that the next generation too would dance, remember, and celebrate.

Proverb at the End: «Dance is the hidden language of the soul of the community.»

Story 5: The Stream's Riddle

The stream in Janja was very special. It splashed and played, and everyone loved it. But one day, the water stopped moving. Instead, there was a big stone in the middle with some words on it:

"Come together and think a bit,
Where water once played and fit.
Four friends can find what's gone,
Work as one, and bring back the dawn."

Everyone looked worried. Lulu said, "What's happened to our stream?"

Mr. Rwego, rubbing his chin, said, "We need to work together to solve this mystery."

The kids felt they should help. Jengo thought of a story about a magical spirit in the water. Amina remembered a song about people helping each other. Kaguru thought of a dance like the water's wiggly waves, and Sitini remembered how the water looked when the sun came up.

Mr. Rwego smiled and said, "Let's use all your ideas!"

So, they stood by the stone, holding hands. Jengo told his story, Amina sang, Kaguru danced, and Sitini drew a picture of the sunrise water on the stone.

Suddenly, the stone moved! Under it was a pretty seashell. Amina blew into the shell, and it made a lovely sound.

And guess what? The water began to move and play again!

Everyone was so happy. Mrs. Rwego said, "It's not just about finding answers. It's about helping each other."

The kids smiled big smiles, knowing that when friends work together, they can solve any problem.

At the end, there was a saying: "Together, we are strong."

Story 6: Mysterious Footprints

Dawn's first light in Janja revealed something most peculiar. Everywhere one looked, there were strange footprints. Neither human nor any recognisable animal, these prints zigzagged through the village, causing quite a stir.

The children were the most excited. «It's a monster!» exclaimed Lulu, her eyes wide.

«Or a friendly giant?» mused Amina, tracing the prints with her fingers.

Kaguru, ever the budding detective, pulled out a small notebook. «We need to follow these,» he declared.

Sitini, skeptical, commented, «What if it's just a prank?»

Regardless of its origin, there was a mystery in Janja, and the village children were more than eager to unravel it. Mrs. Rwego, hearing the commotion, approached the excited group. «Mysterious footprints, you say? How about we solve this puzzle together?»

With a nod from everyone and a makeshift detective hat on Kaguru, the team started their investigation. They followed the prints, making note of their patterns, and trying to decipher any message they might hold.

The footprints led them through the maize fields, past the bubbling stream, up the gentle hill, and finally to the outskirts of Janja, near the dense thicket of trees. Here, the footprints formed a curious circle.

The children, with bated breath, waited for a discovery. Just then, a gentle rustling noise came from the bushes, and out stepped... a baby elephant, its trunk curiously playing with a bucket of paint.

Realisation dawned upon the group. The elephant, having stumbled upon a bucket of paint left outside by Jengo's artist father, had unknowingly painted its path throughout Janja.

Lulu giggled, «Not a monster or a giant, but a little artist!»

Mrs. Rwego laughed, kneeling down to pat the elephant. «Every mystery has an explanation. Sometimes, it's as innocent as a baby elephant's adventure.»

The children, feeling a mix of amusement and relief, decided to name the elephant Pica (Swahili for 'paint'). With Mrs. Rwego's help, they returned the little artist to its herd, but not before Janja had a new story to tell.

Proverb at the End: «What you see is not always what it seems.»

STORY 7: THE LOST KITTEN

The sun was high in the sky when Lulu first heard the soft mewling. Searching around, she found a tiny kitten, its fur matted and eyes filled with fear, hiding behind Mrs. Rwego's famed vegetable patch. Without hesitation, Lulu scooped the kitten into her arms, its soft purrs echoing her heartbeat.

Gathering her friends, she declared, «We must find its home!»

Mr. Rwego, overhearing the commotion, approached the group. With a gentle smile, he said, «A lost kitten in Janja? Let's embark on this mission together.»

Kaguru suggested they ask around the village. «Someone might recognise it,» he pointed out. Sitini thought of making posters, while Amina felt that perhaps the kitten belonged to a neighbouring village.

Following Kaguru's suggestion, the children, with Mr. Rwego leading the way, went door-to-door. At each home, they were met with smiles, a few treats for the kitten, but no owner.

However, as the day progressed, the quest became less about finding the kitten's home and more about the village's overwhelming kindness. Ali Baba offered a small blanket, Mama Sitini crafted a tiny collar, and Jengo's artist father painted a beautiful 'Lost Kitten' sign to place at the village entrance.

By evening, as the golden hues of the setting sun painted Janja, the kitten, surrounded by treats, toys, and a newfound family, looked content. Its purrs resonated with the village's heartbeat.

Seeing this, Mr. Rwego said, «Sometimes, the journey is more important than the destination. Today, we didn't just look for a home; we built one with kindness.»

Amina, hugging the kitten close, whispered, «Welcome to Janja, little one.»

Lulu, with a gleam in her eyes, declared, «Let's name her Zawadi, meaning 'gift' in Swahili. For she's truly a gift that brought Janja even closer.»

The day ended with the children singing lullabies under the vast starry sky, the kitten nestled in their midst, and Janja's heart full of warmth and kindness.

Story 8: Mrs. Rwego's Magic Potion

In Janja, many kids had colds. They were sneezing and coughing.

Kaguru said, "I want to feel better." Sitini nodded, looking sad.

Mrs. Rwego came with a big pot. "I have a special drink to make us feel better!" she said with a smile.

Amina asked, "What's in the drink?"

Mrs. Rwego said, "All good things from our garden!" She put in ginger, which was yellow and smelled nice. Then she added garlic, sweet honey, yellow turmeric, and green moringa leaves.

The drink smelled so good! Mrs. Rwego told the kids how each thing helps them feel better. "Ginger is warm, garlic keeps us strong, honey is sweet and soft, turmeric is like a little helper, and moringa is very special."

Lulu tasted the drink and said, "It's warm and nice!"

Jengo drank and smiled. "It feels like a big hug!"

At the end, there was a saying: "Being kind makes everyone feel good.".»

STORY 9: FESTIVAL OF HARVEST

In Janja, the sun made everything bright and golden. There were big maize plants, beanstalks, and trees full of fruits. It was harvest time, and everyone was happy.

The village was getting ready for a big harvest party. There were colourful decorations everywhere, and the paths were lined with maize and pretty flowers.

Amina, a curious little girl, asked Mr. & Mrs. Rwego, "Why do we have this party?"

Mr. Rwego smiled and said, "We are saying 'thank you' to the earth for all the food."

Mrs. Rwego added, "And we are thankful for everyone who helped and the rain that makes things grow."

Lulu had an idea. "Let's make a Thank You Tree!" With Jengo's help, they made a tree from sticks. They put colourful paper leaves on it. Everyone wrote something they were thankful for on the leaves. "Sunshine," wrote one. "My family," wrote another.

At the party, there was so much food! Everyone sat and ate together. Mrs. Rwego said, "Thank you for the food and for our village."

After eating, they sang and danced. The Thank You Tree looked beautiful in the moonlight. When the party was over, the kids felt very happy and sleepy. They knew being thankful made everything special.

At the end, there was a saying: "Saying 'thank you' makes the heart happy."

STORY 10: WHISPERING WINDS

The children of Janja always believed that the village held secrets. Little did they know, one of those secrets lay in the very winds that caressed their faces, rustled the leaves, and played with their hair.

One breezy afternoon, as the children gathered under the ancient baobab tree, Lulu said, «Do you ever feel the wind speaks?»

Kaguru laughed, «It's just air, Lulu.»

But Mr. Rwego, overhearing their conversation, looked thoughtful. «Lulu might be onto something,» he mused.

Sitini's eyes widened in wonder, «Can the wind really speak, Mr. Rwego?»

Mr. Rwego smiled, «Nature always has messages for us, but we need to learn how to listen.»

And so began the lesson on the Whispering Winds.

Mr. Rwego taught the children to sit silently, close their eyes, and feel the wind on their faces. «Let its coolness seep into your thoughts,» he advised. «Hear its rhythm, feel its pulse.»

For days, the children practiced. While they felt peaceful, they heard no 'whispers'. They grew restless. «Maybe it's just a tale,» Jengo sighed.

One evening, as Amina sat dejectedly, the wind suddenly picked up. It felt like a gentle caress, soothing her worries. She heard... not words, but melodies. Tales of rainforests, of distant mountains, of birds in flight. The wind shared stories of places it had been, of the dreams it carried, of the hopes it sowed.

Amina rushed to tell the others, «I heard it! The whisper!»

The next windy day, each child listened with renewed vigor. And one by one, they started to 'hear'. They shared tales of dancing trees, singing streams, and chirping insects.

Mrs. Rwego, joining them one day, whispered, «Nature doesn't always speak in words. Sometimes, it's a feeling, a tune, or a mere rustle. But to hear, one must have patience.»

The children, their hearts filled with nature's songs, had learned a valuable lesson. In a world of noise, sometimes, it was the softest whispers that held the most profound messages.

Proverb at the End: «To listen closely and reply well is the highest perfection we are able to attain in the art of conversation.»

STORY 11: THE GOLDEN EGG

Golden egg

Janja was abuzz with excitement. Mrs. Rwego's favourite hen, Pendo, had laid a shimmering golden egg. Word spread fast, and soon, villagers and even people from neighbouring villages flocked to see this wonder.

The children, wide-eyed and amazed, gathered around the egg. «It's so shiny!» exclaimed Jengo. Lulu added, «Imagine if Pendo laid a golden egg every day! We'd be the richest village!"

Mr. Rwego, sensing a teachable moment, gathered the children around. «What would you do if you had such a hen?»

Kaguru quickly replied, «I had ask her to lay as many golden eggs as possible!»

35

Sitini, thinking of all the toys she could have, nodded in agreement. Amina daydreamed about building a palace made of gold.

Seeing their excited faces, Mr. Rwego began his tale. «Once, in a land far away, a farmer had a hen that laid a golden egg every day. He became wealthy, but soon, his contentment turned to greed.
He wanted all the gold at once. So, one day, he killed the hen, thinking he'd find a treasure inside.
But there was nothing. He had lost his golden egg and his precious hen.»

The children, engrossed in the tale, looked shocked. Lulu whispered, «He lost everything because of his greed.»

Mrs. Rwego, joining the circle, added, «True wealth isn't in what we have, but in being content with what we have.»

Over the next few days, Pendo continued laying regular eggs. But the children no longer hoped for gold. Instead, they cherished each egg, realising its true value.
One morning, as the golden sun cast its glow over Janja, the golden egg mysteriously hatched, revealing a chick with golden-hued feathers. The chick, named Zawadi, became a symbol of Janja's lesson in contentment.

The children played with Zawadi, their hearts free from the weight of greed. They understood that while gold could buy many things, the joy of simple pleasures, like the chirping of a beloved chick, was truly priceless.

Proverb at the End: «Contentment is natural wealth, luxury is artificial poverty.»

Story 12: The Day Janja Turned Colourful

Dawn broke over Janja, casting a spell of surreal colours. The once-green fields were a brilliant shade of purple, the river shimmered in silver, and the skies...they were a mesmerising blend of pink and gold. Even the animals had changed shades - cows were blue, and chickens sported multi-coloured feathers.

The children of Janja couldn't contain their excitement. They ran through the streets, laughing and pointing at the bizarre transformations. «Look at my green dog!» yelled Jengo, while Sitini showcased her now rainbow-coloured dress.

However, the older villagers were disconcerted. «How will we recognise our crops?» moaned a farmer, pointing at his now-red maize. «Is this a sign of bad luck?» whispered another.

Seeing the mix of joy and confusion, Mrs. Rwego decided it was time to gather the village. As the community sat under the now teal baobab tree, she spoke, «Nature has painted us a picture, a masterpiece that has transformed our everyday life.»

Lulu, wide-eyed, asked, «But why? Why are things so different?»

Mrs. Rwego smiled warmly, «To teach us a lesson. Life is filled with colours - not just in what we see but in who we are. Each colour today represents a culture, a voice, a story. Just as our world is diverse, so now is Janja.» She pointed to the multicolored birds chirping in harmony. «Different shades, but they sing together. Our village, our world, is diverse. Different languages, traditions, stories. But like these colours, they make the world more beautiful.»

Mr. Rwego added, «It's easy to get lost in what we know, to fear what is different. But today, Janja has a chance to see the beauty in diversity, to understand unity.»

As days turned into nights, Janja's vibrant colours remained. The village learned to adapt, finding joy in the newfound diversity. Children made art, farmers exchanged colourful crops, and every evening, villagers gathered to share stories from different cultures, passed down through generations.

STORY 13: SHADOWS IN THE NIGHT

The peaceful village of Janja had always been a haven for its residents. But recently, mysterious shadows began to flit around when the sun went down. Silhouettes of strange creatures, large birds, and eerie figures painted the walls and ground, making children cling to their parents and even adults exchange worried glances.

Rumours spread. Some said the shadows were spirits of ancestors, while others whispered about a curse. Children didn't want to venture out after sunset, and even during the day, they spoke in hushed tones, their games subdued.

One evening, as a group of children sat around a lantern, trying to ward off the looming shadows, Mr. Rwego approached. «Why the long faces?» he asked, though he already knew the answer.

"The shadows, Mr. Rwego. They are scary," Lulu admitted, her voice quivering.

Kaguru added, "We don't know where they come from. They're unknown and frightening."

Mr. Rwego nodded, understanding their fears. "How about we investigate together?" he proposed.

With a mixture of apprehension and curiosity, the children agreed. Armed with lanterns and torches, and led by Mr. Rwego, they ventured into the night.

As they approached one of the shadows, Mr. Rwego pointed his torch to its origin. A simple scarecrow, with outstretched arms, was casting a long, exaggerated shadow. Further along, the large bird shadow was caused by a feather duster swinging in the wind.

One by one, the fearsome shadows were revealed to be ordinary objects distorted by the play of light and darkness.

Seeing the relief on the children's faces, Mr. Rwego said, "Fears are often like these shadows. Unknown, magnified, and intimidating. But when we shine a light on them, when we try to understand and face them, they often turn out to be much smaller and more manageable than we imagined."

The children, now fearless, played with the shadows, making shapes with their hands and laughing at the once-intimidating silhouettes.

Word spread through Janja about Mr. Rwego and the children's night time adventure. The village soon started 'Shadow Festivals,' where they played with lights and objects, turning fear into fun.

From that day on, the children of Janja not only slept peacefully but also dreamt of dancing with the shadows, understanding that the key to facing fears was to shine a light on them.

Proverb at the End: «Fear diminishes as understanding grows.»

When Janja finally returned to its original hues, its spirit remained colourful. Children now played new games, elders exchanged tales of old, and the village festivals became a melting pot of traditions.

The day Janja turned colourful was a day it never forgot. Not because of the magical transformation of its landscape, but for the unity and understanding it brought among its people.

Story 14: The Tale of Akavumbura

Evening in Janja was always a special time. As the sun began its descent, painting the sky with hues of orange and purple, families would gather around, sharing stories and preparing for a restful night. But for Mrs. Rwego, the evenings were a bit challenging, especially when it came to putting her youngest, Malaika, to bed.

Unlike the other children of her age, Malaika was full of boundless energy and a burning curiosity. «Why is the sky blue? Why do fireflies glow? Why do we need to sleep?» were just a few of the many questions she posed. But of all, the toughest was, «Why do I have to go to bed now?»

One such evening, as Mrs. Rwego tried to coax Malaika to bed, she whispered a tale her grandmother had once told her. «Have you ever heard of Akavumbura, dear?»

Malaika's eyes widened with interest. «No, who's that?»

Mrs. Rwego glanced around and leaned in, her voice low and mysterious. «Akavumbura is a creature of the night, an old spirit from the tales of Janja. When the village is asleep, Akavumbura comes out, wandering the streets, listening for the sounds of children who are still awake.»

Malaika gulped. «What does it do?»

Mrs. Rwego continued, «Akavumbura seeks out children who aren't in bed, those who disobey their parents. And if it finds them... it gives them a little bite. The bite isn't harmful but it's said to be very ticklish, making the child giggle. And the strangest part? If the child cries out, no one can hear. Only when morning comes, and the child tells the tale, do the parents realise what happened.»

Malaika looked thoughtful. «So, if I go to bed, Akavumbura won't visit?»

Mrs. Rwego nodded, tucking her in. «Exactly. Akavumbura only visits children who are still up and about.»

That night, Malaika, though still curious, didn't want to meet Akavumbura. She snuggled under her blankets, and in no time, she was deep in slumber.

As days turned to weeks, Malaika's bedtime routine became easier. She would still ask a myriad of questions during the day, but come bedtime, she'd remember the tale of Akavumbura and drift into sleep.

The other parents in Janja soon heard about Mrs. Rwego's creative solution and began sharing the story with their children. It wasn't just a tale to induce sleep but a story about respecting routines and the wisdom of elders.

Proverb at the End: «In every ancient tale, there's a lesson for the present.»

Story 15: The Village Time Capsule

In Janja, everyone was gathering under a big tree. They looked at Mr. & Mrs. Rwego, who were holding a big wooden box.

Mr. Rwego said, "Kids, this box is like a treasure map to the future!"

The kids looked puzzled. "What do you mean?"

Mrs. Rwego explained, "It's a special box where we put things from today. We will bury it. Then, many, many years from now, people will open it to see what life was like today."

Everyone in the village wanted to put something in the box. Jengo added his favourite toy car. Lulu drew a picture of Janja and added it. Some families wrote letters with stories.

The day came to close the box. Mr. Rwego put an old picture of Janja inside, and Mrs. Rwego added a pretty necklace.

Everyone watched as the box was put in a deep hole and covered with dirt.

Mrs. Rwego said, "This box tells a story about us, our village, and our love for Janja."

Mr. Rwego added, "One day, our grandkids will find this box and learn all about us."

Even after a very long time, people in Janja remembered the special box and the stories about it.

And in Janja, the box became a way to remember the past and look forward to the future.

At the end, there was a saying: "Remembering the past helps us dream for the future."

Story 16: Mrs. Rwego's Flying Garden

In the village of Janja, everyone woke up to a big surprise. Mrs. Rwego's garden was flying in the air!

All the kids ran to see. Kito tried to jump up to touch it. Sana laid down and looked at its shadow.

Malaika asked, "Mrs. Rwego, why is your garden flying?"

Mrs. Rwego smiled, "It's magic and imagination!"

She let the kids step onto the edge of the garden. It felt soft and bouncy. They saw sunflowers and pumpkins up close in the air.

Jengo asked, "So you used magic to make it fly?"

Mrs. Rwego laughed, "I dreamed of a flying garden and used some tricks to make it look like it's flying. But the real magic is in our imagination and the fun we have."

The kids played in the flying garden all day, pretending they were in a special world where everything floated.

At night, they told stories about their fun day in the flying garden and other things they wished could fly.

The story ends with a saying: "Dreaming big lets us touch the sky."

STORY 17: THE LEAP TO FRIENDSHIP

In the heart of Janja, in the homestead of Mr. & Mrs. Rwego, a peculiar quarrel was ongoing. Each day, just as the village settled into its routine, a series of barks and meows would echo, signalling yet another disagreement between Paka, the family cat, and Mbwa, the spirited dog.

While the elders had grown used to this daily ruckus, Nia, Mrs. Rwego's youngest, couldn't bear it. «Why do they always shout and quarrel?» she often wondered aloud.

One sunny afternoon, Nia decided she had had enough. She sat both Paka and Mbwa down, a considerable feat in itself. Looking them squarely in their eyes, she asked, «Why do you two always fight? What is the root of your disagreement?»

Of course, neither Paka nor Mbwa could articulate their feelings, but their guilty glances and drooped tails spoke volumes.

With a determined nod, Nia announced, «It's clear you both need a distraction, a game that doesn't involve chasing or hissing.» And with that, she pondered for a moment before her face lit up with an idea.

She demonstrated by crouching low to the ground and then leaping up high, arms outstretched. «It's called the Jump-Up game! The one who jumps the highest without making a sound wins!»

Paka and Mbwa looked at each other, puzzled but intrigued. Nia encouraged Mbwa first. With a playful bark, the dog tried to mimic her, jumping up with all his might. Paka, not to be outdone, followed suit, leaping gracefully into the air.

Hours passed, and the two were engrossed in their new game. Every leap was a challenge, every silent landing a victory. For the first time, they were not competing against each other but were united in a mutual goal. Days turned into weeks, and the village of Janja soon bore witness to a heart warming sight – Paka and Mbwa, once arch-nemeses, now leaped together in joyous harmony. Their daily quarrels had turned into playful jumps, and the once echoing shouts had transformed into the soft thud of paws landing on the earth.

Mrs. Rwego, observing from a distance, smiled at Nia's ingenious solution. Nia had taught the village a valuable lesson - that confrontation could be turned into cooperation with just a change in perspective.

Proverb at the End: «To change the dance, one must change the tune.»

STORY 18 THE TALE OF THE TAILLESS FROG

In the green village of Janja, long before the Rwego family came, there was a wise creature named Mana. Mana was like a guardian angel, watching over all the animals and birds.

One sunny day, Mana had a box full of beautiful tails. She called Kiboko, the frog, and said, "Kiboko, I want you to give these tails to our animal friends."

Kiboko was excited! He hopped from one animal to another, giving each one a shiny, new tail. The monkey got a long tail, the rabbit got a fluffy tail, and the bird got a feathery tail.

But as the day went on, the box of tails became empty. Kiboko had given tails to all the animals and birds, but he forgot one thing. He forgot to save a tail for himself!

Kiboko looked at his back and realized he didn't have a tail. Feeling a little sad, he went back to Mana and said, "Mana, I gave tails to everyone, but I forgot to keep one for myself."

Mana smiled kindly and said, "Kiboko, you were so generous and thoughtful, but I don't have any more tails left."

That's why, to this day, frogs in Janja don't have tails. But every time the animals see Kiboko, they remember his kindness and how he put others before himself. And in Janja, that's more special than any tail.

Story 19: The Dinner Dilemma in Janja"

In the lush village of Janja, there was a crocodile named Croco who lived in the reserve waters. Nearby in the jungle, there was a shiny monkey named Momo who loved to jump from tree to tree, enjoying the weather.

One sunny day, Momo spotted Croco sunbathing by the water and thought, "Why not make a new friend?" He hopped down and introduced himself. They chatted for hours, laughing and sharing stories. Soon, they became the best of friends.

Momo lived in a cozy hut with a nice table and four chairs. Wanting to share a meal with his new friend, he invited Croco over for dinner. When Croco arrived, Momo proudly pointed to a chair, "Please, have a seat!"

Croco tried and tried, but his big tail and legs made it impossible to sit on the small chairs. Feeling a bit embarrassed and unhappy, Croco decided to head back to his reserve waters.

A few days later, Croco thought of a way to return the gesture. He invited Momo to his home in the lake for a special fish barbecue. Momo, curious and excited, accepted the invitation.

When Momo arrived, he was surprised to see Croco's table - it was a large flat rock beside the water. Before they ate, Croco handed Momo a large soap. "First, we wash our hands," he said.

Momo tried to wash his hands, but no matter how much he scrubbed, they still looked dark and shiny. Momo began to worry. "What if Croco thinks my hands are dirty and decides I might make a good meal instead?"

Thinking quickly, Momo had an idea. "Oh, Croco! I forgot my special soap at home. It's called Omo and it's the only soap that works for my shiny hands. Could you take me back to get it?"

Croco, wanting to be a good host, agreed. He let Momo climb onto his back and started to swim towards the Janja jungle.

As soon as they reached the edge of the jungle, Momo hopped off, scampered up a tree, and called out, "Bye bye, Croco! Thanks for the ride!" He knew it was better to be safe than sorry.

And so, while they remained friends, Momo and Croco decided that maybe it was best to hang out in places where they both felt comfortable. After all, friendship is about understanding and respecting each other's differences.

Story 20: Peter's Day at Home

In the neighbouring village to Janja, there lived a hardworking man named Peter. He shared a cozy home with his loving wife, Mary, and their spirited toddler. Every day, as the sun peeked over the horizon, Peter would set out for the fields while Mary managed the home, ensuring everything was in order and looking after their young calf.

One sunny afternoon, Peter returned home, his stomach growling loudly. He was surprised to find no food ready and asked Mary, "What happened? Why isn't lunch ready?"

Mary, tired from the day's chores, tried to explain all the tasks she had managed. However, Peter, clouded by his hunger, wasn't convinced. "It can't be that hard," he muttered.

Seeing an opportunity to teach Peter a lesson, Mary suggested, "Let's swap roles tomorrow. You manage the home, and I'll work in the fields."

Confident in his abilities, Peter agreed.

The following day, Mary left early for the fields, while Peter tried his best to handle the domestic chores. The mischievous calf, not used to Peter's ways, began mooing incessantly. Wanting to multitask, Peter thought of a clever idea. He tied the calf to a long rope, slung it through the ceiling, and tied the other end to his leg. This way, he could ensure the calf grazed on the rooftop grass without wandering off, while he attended to the house.

However, a few minutes later, the restless calf decided the rooftop wasn't for her. She took a daring leap off the roof, and as she descended, the rope tugged sharply at Peter's leg. Before he knew it, Peter found himself dangling from the ceiling, his world upside down!

Mary returned home to find a house in chaos. The dishes were unwashed, the laundry was everywhere, the toddler was crying, and in the midst of it all, her husband was hanging from the ceiling, a perplexed look on his face.

With a mix of concern and a hint of a smile, Mary set things right, gently lowering Peter and comforting their child.

That evening, as they sat down to dinner, Peter looked at Mary, gratitude in his eyes. "You do so much every day," he acknowledged, "and I never realized just how challenging it can be."

Mary smiled, squeezing his hand. "It's all in a day's work," she replied, both understanding the value of each other's roles a little better.

From that day on, Peter never underestimated the challenges of managing a home. He had learned his lesson in the most unexpected of ways!

Story 21: George's Silly Adventures

In a village near Mr. and Mrs. Rwegos' home, there was a boy named George who lived with his mum, Mrs. Barnett. George always wanted to be helpful, but sometimes, his ideas got him into funny situations!

One sunny day, while George's dad was away, Mrs. Barnett needed a needle for her sewing machine. "George," she said, "could you ride your scooter to the Rwegos' house and borrow a needle for me?"

George was excited. He hopped on his scooter, but on his way back, he accidentally dropped the needle! "Oh no!" he thought and got an idea to burn the nearby bushes so he could search in the ashes. But, he still couldn't find it.

Returning home, George showed his empty hands. Mrs. Barnett was surprised. "George! Why didn't you use your pocket to keep the needle safe?"

Trying to make things right, Mrs. Barnett then asked him to borrow a hoe from the Rwegos. To carry it easily, George made a big hole in his shirt to hold the hoe and rode his scooter. When his mum saw the ruined shirt, she exclaimed, "George! Why didn't you just push your scooter and carry the hoe properly?"

Next, she asked George to bring their little piggy from the yard. Imagining he was doing it the right way, George pushed his scooter with one hand and carried the piggy on his shoulder with the other. Mrs. Barnett just laughed, "Oh, George! You and your funny ways!"

That evening, they heard noises outside. To be safe, they decided to hide. As they hid, a group of sneaky raccoons came to play and left shiny objects around. George, thinking quickly, distracted them with some crumbs.

As they scampered away, George and his mum discovered the raccoons had left behind shiny buttons, sparkling stones, and other treasures. Laughing, they went inside, with George saying, "Mum, every day is an adventure with us!"

And Mrs. Barnett replied, "Yes, George, especially with your silly ideas!"

Story 22: Goodbye, Janja

The sun cast its golden hue over the village of Janja, painting the mud-brick walls with a warm glow. Children were buzzing with excitement, their laughter and chatter filling the air. The graduation ceremony of Janja's nursery school was upon them, marking both an end and a beginning.

As parents proudly adjusted their children's graduation hats and robes, Mr. & Mrs. Rwego stood at the centre of it all, their eyes gleaming with pride and a hint of melancholy. They had watched these children grow, teaching them the values and lessons that the village held dear.

Malaika, ever the spirited one, exclaimed, «I don't want to leave Janja's nursery! I want to stay here forever.»

Lulu, holding back tears, agreed, «Me too. Everything will change now.»

Mrs. Rwego, overhearing their conversation, beckoned them over. «Change,» she began gently, «is like the changing seasons. Just as the bare trees of winter give way to the blossoms of spring, each phase of our life has its own beauty and lessons.»

«But we love it here,» protested Jengo, his voice quivering.

Mr. Rwego knelt, placing a hand on Jengo's shoulder. «We love having you here. But just as a bird must leave its nest to soar high, you must move forward to achieve great things. Janja's nursery school was your nest, and now the world is waiting for you to spread your wings.»

The children gathered around the Rwegos, seeking comfort and understanding. Mrs. Rwego, ever the storyteller, began, «Do you remember the story of the caterpillar?»

Nods all around.

«It wraps itself in a cocoon, away from the world. But then, it emerges as a beautiful butterfly, ready to explore the vastness of the world. You are like that butterfly. Janja's nursery was your cocoon, nurturing and safe. But now, you are ready to explore, learn, and grow.»

The ceremony began, and one by one, the children were called to the stage to receive their graduation certificates. With each name called, cheers erupted, marking their achievements and the journey ahead.

As the sun began to set, casting long shadows across Janja, the children, now graduates, released balloons into the sky. Each balloon carried a note, a dream, a wish for the future.

And as the balloons drifted higher, the children realised that while they were saying goodbye to a cherished chapter, they were also greeting a world filled with endless possibilities.

With Mr. & Mrs. Rwego's teachings etched in their hearts, they were ready to embrace change and grow into the best versions of themselves.

Proverb at the End: «Every ending is a new beginning; we only need the courage to turn the page.»

Printed in Great Britain
by Amazon